SMASHING LUMPKINS

CARTOON NETWORK®

by Paul Siefken

"THE P⟨   ⟩"

as created ⟨   ⟩

SCHOLASTIC INC.

New York   Toronto   London   Auckland   Sydney
Mexico City   New Delhi   Hong Kong   Buenos Aires

ISBN 0-439-29594-7

Copyright © 2001 by Cartoon Network.
CARTOON NETWORK, the logo, THE POWERPUFF GIRLS and all related characters and elements are trademarks of and © Cartoon Network.
(s01)

Published by Scholastic Inc. All rights reserved.
SCHOLASTIC and associated logos are trademarks and/or registered trademarks of Scholastic Inc.

Designed by Peter Koblish

Illustrated by Tom LaPadula

12 11 10 9 8 7 6 5 4 3   1 2 3 4 5 6/0

Printed in the U.S.A.
First Scholastic printing, December 2001

SUGAR . . .

SPICE . . .

AND EVERYTHING NICE . . .

These were the ingredients chosen to

create the perfect little girl.

But Professor Utonium accidentally

added an extra ingredient to

the concoction —

CHEMICAL X:

And thus, The Powerpuff Girls were born!

Using their ultra superpowers,

BLOSSOM,

BUBBLES,

and **BUTTERCUP**

have dedicated their lives to fighting crime

and the forces of evil!

chapter 1

The city of Townsville! A city with class and style, where fine art and beautiful music are loved by all, especially The Powerpuff Girls. . . . Well, at least by Professor Utonium. It was a quiet, peaceful evening, and the Professor decided to give Blossom, Bubbles, and Buttercup a musical treat.

"Girls, I have a surprise for you tonight. While you get ready for bed, I'm going to play your favorite classical music on the stereo," said the Professor.

"That's a great idea, Professor," said Blossom. "It will help us unwind after a long day of fighting crime."

"Classical music is boring," Buttercup told her sisters as they floated upstairs to get ready for bed. "My favorite music is classic rock!"

"I know, but classical music is good, too," said Blossom. "It's relaxing."

"I'll say," Bubbles agreed. "The Professor's music sure makes me sleepy."

Thanks to their superpowers, The Powerpuff Girls could get ready for bed faster than regular children. By the time the Professor started the music, the Girls had already brushed their teeth, changed into their pajamas, and hopped into bed.

Because they worked so hard to keep Townsville safe from monsters and villains, the Girls also fell asleep faster than anyone else. Sure enough, after only a few notes, their eyelids began to droop. By the time the Professor had come to the Girls' room to tuck them in, they were already sound asleep.

"Good night, my little superheroes," whispered the Professor. He turned out the light and left the door open a crack, just the way Bubbles liked it.

The Powerpuff Girls were enjoying a well-deserved slumber. All snug in their bed, they didn't look like tough super-heroes at all. They just looked like ordi-nary little girls. But ordinary girls can't stop a three-headed, fire-breathing fish

dragon from eating the Townsville Bank. And that's just what The Powerpuff Girls had done earlier that day.

Now, however, all was calm and perfectly still. The only sound to be heard was the Girls' steady breathing.

But what's this? Something seems to be disturbing The Powerpuff Girls. Blossom's eyes are fluttering. Bubbles's pigtails are twitching! Buttercup's fists are pumping! What could be bugging them on such a peaceful night?

Suddenly, all three Girls sat up in bed.

"What's that awful sound?" asked Blossom.

"I don't know, but it's driving me crazy!" cried Buttercup.

"It's coming from outside," said Bubbles.

"Let's go check it out," Blossom suggested.

The Powerpuff Girls flew out the window into the night. The noise didn't seem to be bothering anyone else in the neighborhood. All the lights were out. Everything was peaceful. Except for that terrible sound!

"We must be the only ones who can hear it," said Blossom.

"Lucky us," Buttercup grumbled.

The Girls used their superhearing to

track the noise to its source. As they got closer to the outskirts of town, the noise got louder. And harder to bear! By the time they reached the woods, The Powerpuff Girls could barely hear themselves think.

Suddenly, the noisy culprit appeared through a clearing in the trees. It was that troublemaking backwoods brute, Fuzzy Lumpkins! He was sitting on his porch, playing his banjo and singing. But the noise he was making really couldn't be called music.

I gots me a pig by th' name o' Roy,
An' that ole hog, he's a good ole boy.

I likes ta take 'at feller down by th' lake.
We's gonna catch us a mean ole snake,
Swing 'im round by his rattlin' tail,
Cook 'im in a pan wit' a mess o' snails . . .

"That's the worst song I've ever heard!" shouted Buttercup.

Fuzzy stopped playing and looked up. "Who's 'at on ma property?" he screamed.

"It's us!" said Blossom.

"The Powerpuff Girls!" said Buttercup.

"Hiya, Fuzzy!" called Bubbles.

"Y'all git on outta here!" shouted Fuzzy. "I's got more singin' ta do."

"We're sorry to bother you, Fuzzy," said Bubbles. "But your music is keeping us awake."

"Would you mind keeping it down?"

asked Blossom. "Or could you possibly wait until morning to play?"

"What's a matter, Powerpuff Girls? Is ma singin' keepin' y'all littl'uns from gettin' your beauty rest?" Fuzzy chuckled. "Well, too bad! I don't like you meddlin' superheroes nohow. Now git!"

"That does it," said Buttercup. "Let's get him!"

"Wait, Buttercup! We can't beat up Fuzzy just for singing, even if he does sound terrible," reasoned Blossom. "We'll just have to hope that he gets tired soon so we can sleep."

"Can we ask him to sing about puppies and butterflies instead of pigs and snakes?" asked Bubbles.

"I'm afraid not," said Blossom.

So the sleepy Powerpuff Girls flew back home, and Fuzzy Lumpkins went back to making his horrible hillbilly music.

Oh, no! The Girls can't fight crime without any rest! What are they going to do? Fuzzy better stop singing soon . . . or at least take some banjo lessons.

Chapter 2

The Powerpuff Girls were very cranky when they came to breakfast the next morning. Fuzzy's playing and singing had kept them up all night.

"Good morning," said the Professor. "Isn't it a beautiful day, Girls?"

"Whatever," said Buttercup. "What's for breakfast?"

"I've made chocolate chip pancakes," the Professor announced proudly. "Those are your favorite, aren't they, Bubbles?"

"Huh?" Bubbles mumbled. "I don't know. I'm not really that hungry."

"What about you, Blossom? Would you like some good hearty sausages to give you strength to take on the day's challenges?" asked the Professor.

"Look, Professor," Blossom answered. "You can stop acting so cheery. We're grumpy because we didn't get any sleep last night. Fuzzy Lumpkins kept us up all night with his stupid music."

"That's funny," said the Professor. "I didn't hear anything."

"Of course you didn't," snapped Buttercup. "You don't have superhearing."

"Well, I'm sorry you had a rough

night," said the Professor. "But I don't like your attitude. Taking your troubles out on others doesn't help anything. Now finish your breakfast and get ready for school."

The Powerpuff Girls looked ashamed. They dragged themselves upstairs to get ready for school.

This isn't right! The Powerpuff Girls talking back to the Professor! What could be next? They better wake up and smell the pancakes, or they're in for a heap of trouble at school!

Later that day, at Pokey Oaks Kindergarten, Ms. Keane was teaching her class about flowers.

"Flowers come in many shapes, sizes, and colors," said Ms. Keane. "Would someone like to draw a flower for me on the blackboard?"

Blossom's friend Mary volunteered. She went to the board and drew a big, pretty daisy.

"Very good, Mary," said Ms. Keane. "Would anyone else like to try?"

Elmer Sglue, who liked to eat paste, raised his sticky hand. He went to the front of the class and drew a tulip on the blackboard.

"That's great," said Ms. Keane. "Bubbles, I know flowers are one of your favorite things to draw. Bubbles?" Ms. Keane looked around the room. Bubbles was asleep in back, at her desk. So were her two sisters.

"Bubbles, wake up, dear. It's not nap time yet. Wouldn't you like to draw a flower for us?" Ms. Keane asked.

"No, I'm too tired to draw," said Bubbles groggily.

Too tired to draw! This is worse than I thought. If Bubbles is too tired to draw, how will she ever defend Townsville?

When the Girls got home from school, they went straight to bed. But the moment their heads hit their pillows, the hotline buzzed. Townsville was in trouble!

Blossom slowly dragged herself to the phone. "Hello," she said wearily. "Ahh, do we have to? Okay. We're coming."

"What is it now?" asked Buttercup.

"It was the Mayor," said Blossom. "The Gangreen Gang is destroying the supermarket. The Mayor wants us to clean up the aisles. Come on, Girls, we better go."

The Powerpuff Girls flew to the supermarket as fast as their tired superpowers could take them.

The supermarket was a mess. Big Billy had eaten all of the chips in aisle five. Grubber had drooled all over the deli section. Snake had touched all the fruit with his slithery fingers. Little Arturo had pulled all the prizes out of the cereal boxes. And Ace, the gang's leader, was taking the money out of the cash registers!

"Not so . . . (yawn) . . . fast, Gangreen Gang," Blossom said slowly.

"Look who it is — The Powerpuff Brats," Ace cackled. "What do you want, Blossom, paper or plastic?"

Before Blossom could respond, Billy grabbed her and threw her

toward Ace, who caught her in a paper shopping bag.

"Paper, I guess," Ace laughed.

Seeing Blossom bagged gave Bubbles and Buttercup a wake-up call. They sprang into action.

Buttercup rocketed toward Billy, hitting his stomach like a battering ram. Billy went sailing into the aisles, knocking them down like dominoes.

"Cleanup on aisles two, three, four, and five," announced Buttercup.

Next, Bubbles got into the action. She grabbed Little Arturo and rolled him like a bowling ball, straight at Grubber. They collided with a thunderous crash and were buried under a mound of fresh apples.

"I think we have a couple of bad apples in that bunch," said Bubbles.

Snake was pulling money out of the last

cash register when Blossom burst out of the bag and smashed his face into a price scanner. "Price check on a ninety-pound bag of slime!" she called out.

When The Powerpuff Girls got home, they climbed into bed and fell asleep immediately. And that's when they heard it.

Oh, them Powerpuff Girls cain't bother me none,
I's jus' sittin' here playin' fer fun.
Ain't nothin' I likes more than causin' them pain,
Makin' 'em suffer till the day is done.

Fuzzy was singing again! And this time, he was making fun of them.

The Powerpuff Girls had enough! They flew over to Fuzzy's house faster than they

had ever flown, and took Fuzzy by surprise.

"Try singing with a mouthful of knuckle sandwich!" Buttercup shouted. She punched Fuzzy so hard that he went flying across his run-down old shack.

"Let's see you play your banjo without any strings!" screamed Bubbles. She yanked the strings from Fuzzy's banjo.

"And now for the big finish," said Blossom. She swung Fuzzy's banjo like a baseball bat, smashing it into a hundred pieces that scattered throughout the little cabin.

Exhausted, The Powerpuff Girls flew home and went straight to sleep, leaving Fuzzy in stunned silence. But he wouldn't stay silent for long.

That doesn't sound good! You did it this time, Girls! Fuzzy's going to be pretty mad about your breaking his banjo. Sleep while you can, Girls. Sleep while you can!

chapter 3

Fuzzy Lumpkins sat on the porch in silence all night long. He looked at the broken pieces of his banjo scattered all over his cabin. And as he sat and looked, his anger grew . . . and grew . . . and grew!

At the crack of dawn, Fuzzy's rooster, Bubba, crowed.

"That's jus' what I was a-thinkin', Bubba," declared Fuzzy. "I'm so mad at them Powerpuff Girls that I could crow ma head off. I gotta git them Girls back for smashin' up ma banjo. But how?"

Bubba crowed again loudly.

"Gawlly, Bubba, ya don't need to be so loud about it," replied Fuzzy. But that gave him an idea.

"Them Powerpuff Girls hates ma music so much that they went to smashin' ma banjo," said Fuzzy. "Now I'm gonna do some smashin' of ma own!"

Fuzzy stood up and marched straight into downtown Townsville. He stopped outside the Townsville Music Store. In the window was the biggest, shiniest, loudest-looking electric guitar that he had ever seen.

"That there guitar is jus' what I need," shouted Fuzzy. "Time fer some smashin'!" And with that, Fuzzy smashed the window of the music store and grabbed the electric guitar.

Fuzzy Lumpkins with an electric guitar! My ears hurt already. The Powerpuff Girls are in for a long, loud day! Hey, where are The Powerpuff Girls, anyway? Oh, it's a school day. That means they must be at . . . Pokey Oaks Kindergarten!

After a long night of rest, The Powerpuff Girls were back to their cheerful selves.

Bubbles was drawing lots of flowers on the blackboard. "Look, Ms. Keane," called Bubbles. "I drew a daisy and a daffodil and a lily and a pansy and a puppy!"

"They're beautiful, Bubbles," said Ms. Keane.

Blossom was helping Elmer Sglue with his letters. "See, Elmer, it's a lot easier to write when your hands aren't so sticky," she explained.

And Buttercup was building a mini Townsville out of blocks. "The city of Townsville," Buttercup narrated. "It was a peaceful day when out of nowhere a giant monster started destroying everything!

Rowr!" Buttercup knocked the blocks to the floor.

Everything was back to normal.

But suddenly, a terrible sound filled the classroom. It was loud. It rattled the windows. It shook the walls. It screeched and it howled and it whined!

"Hurray! A fire drill!" shouted Bubbles. "Form a single-file line and don't run."

"It's not a fire drill, Bubbles," said Buttercup. "This noise is way too loud!"

"Then what is it, Ms. Smarty Pants?" asked Bubbles as loud as she could.

"I don't know. But it's not a fire drill," Buttercup yelled back.

"Don't worry, Ms. Keane," Blossom screamed. "We'll get to the bottom of this."

But Ms. Keane wasn't listening to Blossom. She was listening to the noise. In fact, she was tapping her feet and bobbing her head. Then she started dancing! Everyone in the classroom was dancing! But this wasn't a normal dance. It was some kind of *smash dance*!

Mary was stomping on crayons! Elmer was throwing his paste! Harry was smushing the art clay! Even Ms. Keane was crunching her colored chalk!

"Why is everybody acting so crazy?" Blossom called to her sisters.

"I don't know," yelled Buttercup. "But it looks kind of fun!"

"Don't be silly, Buttercup," Blossom shouted. "We need to figure out what's making all that noise."

"But how can we tell where it's coming from?" asked Bubbles. "It's too loud."

"Maybe the Professor can help," said Blossom. "Let's go ask him."

The Powerpuff Girls took off toward home, leaving the wild classroom behind.

Let's hope the Professor can help! And quickly! The kids are poking holes in Pokey Oaks!

Chapter 4

As The Powerpuff Girls rocketed across the sky, they looked down over the city of Townsville. Everywhere they glanced, people were dancing and smashing everything in sight!

The Girls listened carefully to the noise. But they couldn't figure out where it was coming from. It seemed to be everywhere! But how?

By the time they got home, The Powerpuff Girls had splitting headaches.

Don't worry, Girls! The Professor will find a solution. He's always under control. I'm sure this crazy music isn't getting to him.

Inside the house, the noise was even louder.

"It sounds like it's coming from the Professor's lab," Blossom shouted.

"I hope the Professor is okay," Bubbles worried.

The three Girls flew like a shot to the Professor's lab. It was a wreck!

Sparks flew from smashed computers. Chemicals spilled from broken beakers. Laser beams shot across the room, destroying everything in their path.

And in the middle of all the destruction was the Professor. Dancing and smashing! Smashing and dancing! The Professor was destroying his own lab!

"What are you doing, Professor?" shouted Bubbles.

"Let me try," said Blossom. "Professor, calm down! Listen to me! Townsville's in trouble, and we need your help!"

But the Professor just kept dancing.

Finally, Buttercup took action. She flew over to the Professor and lifted him off his feet.

"Put me down, Buttercup," said the Professor. "I want to dance and smash!"

"But why?" asked Blossom.

"Haven't you heard?" asked the Professor. "It's the hot new dance! It's all over the radio! It's everywhere! It's the Smashing Lumpkins!" The Professor proudly displayed the T-shirt he had on under his lab coat.

"Smashing Lumpkins!?" The Powerpuff Girls cried out.

"It figures Fuzzy has something to do with this mess," said Blossom.

"I guess smashing his banjo didn't teach him his lesson," said Buttercup.

"Let's go pay our friend Fuzzy another visit," said Blossom.

Buttercup and Blossom took off. But they stopped in midair just before they crashed through the ceiling. Bubbles wasn't with them.

She was floating next to the Professor with a strange look on her face.

"What's wrong, Bubbles?" asked Blossom.

"Do you hear something funny?" Bubbles asked.

"Of course we hear something, Bubbles!" cried Buttercup. "It's Fuzzy! Haven't you been paying attention?"

"Not Fuzzy's music," said Bubbles. "It sounds different. It sounds like . . ."

"The hotline!" shouted Blossom. She

looked across the room and saw the light on the Powerpuff phone blinking. "Way to go, Bubbles." Blossom zipped over to answer it.

"Hello!" she said. "What's that? Is that you, Mayor? I can't hear you. There's too much noise. What did you say? You need us to block the cold? Put the clock on hold? Your socks have mold?"

"No, no, no!" shouted the Mayor, on the other end of the line. "I said, it's time to *rock 'n' roll!*"

Then Blossom heard a loud crash, and the phone went dead.

"Who was that?" asked Bubbles.

"It was the Mayor," Blossom answered. "And I think we better head downtown."

"Why? Is that where Fuzzy is?" asked Buttercup.

"I don't know about Fuzzy," Blossom said. "But the Mayor just told me that it was time to rock 'n' roll!"

"Rock 'n' roll!" shouted the Professor.

"I want the old Professor back," said Bubbles, frowning.

"Me, too," said Blossom. "But we better get downtown to see if we can help the Mayor first."

"Let's roll!" shouted Buttercup. The Girls blasted off toward downtown Townsville.

Better hurry, Girls! Or there won't be much left of Townsville to save!

Chapter 5

In downtown Townsville, there was a huge crowd assembled in front of City Hall. Everyone was doing the same smash dance as the Professor and Ms. Keane and the kids at school. But this time, someone was leading them in song.

Fuzzy Lumpkins was standing at the top of the steps to City Hall. He was playing a bright red electric guitar. Fuzzy played his guitar loudly. He played it fast. And he played it badly!

The crowd was shouting his name over and over again. "Fuzzy! Fuzzy! Fuzzy!"

"It looks like a rock 'n' roll concert!" shouted Buttercup.

"But Fuzzy's the worst guitar player ever," said Bubbles. "No wonder everybody's acting so crazy."

But Fuzzy didn't just play his guitar. He also used it to smash things. And as he smashed, he sang a terrible song.

Smash! Crash! Bash some glass!
Rob th' bank 'n' take th' cash!
Fuzzy ain't got no time fer nice,
I jus' wants ta break things twice.
Hit stuff with a big ole stick,
Give somethin' a great big kick.
If 'n you jus' cain't rock enough
Take a rock and smash some stuff!

"Why are people listening to him? He's awful!" shouted Blossom.

"Because it's cool to be cruel!" the Mayor answered from behind them.

The Mayor was helping the Gangreen Gang spray-paint graffiti on the walls of City Hall.

"What are you guys doing here?" Blossom asked the Gangreen Gang. "We busted you at the Townsville Supermarket yesterday. Shouldn't you still be in jail?"

"I let them out for bad behavior," said the Mayor. "Come on, Girls, break something! It's fun. See?"

The Mayor pulled the key to the city out of his coat. He threw it at one of City Hall's windows, and the window broke with a loud smash!

"Fuzzy's music is making everybody think it's okay to destroy things," said Blossom.

"Let's pull the plug!" shouted Buttercup.

"But everybody loves his music," said Bubbles. "Won't they be mad?"

"Not if we sing them a happy song," said Blossom.

The Powerpuff Girls flew over to Fuzzy and unplugged his guitar.

"What in tarnation are you doin'?" complained Fuzzy.

"Your singing days are over, Fuzzy," said Blossom. She took the microphone from his hand.

"Booo! Booo!" the crowd shouted.

What's this? The people of Townsville have turned against The Powerpuff Girls! Say it isn't so!

"People of Townsville!" Blossom called into the microphone. "Wouldn't you rather hear a happy song?"

"No!" shouted the crowd. "We want to smash something!"

"But don't you like songs about puppies and butterflies and rainbows?" Bubbles asked.

"No!" the crowd shouted again.

"Well, we're going to sing for you anyway," said Buttercup. "Hit it, Girls!"

And The Powerpuff Girls began to sing:

Play! Run! Have some fun!
Smell the flowers in the sun!
The Powerpuff Girls want you to know
We all have a big kiss to throw.
Find your friend and give a hug
Because all we really need is love!

As The Powerpuff Girls sang, the crowd began to calm down! They stopped shouting! They stopped smashing things! They stopped dancing by themselves and started dancing with one another. People were smiling! People were laughing! The people of Townsville were back to normal.

Isn't this great? It looks like it's time to say

those words again: So once again, the day is saved, thanks to . . . wait a second. What's Ace doing over there with the microphone cord?

Ace pulled a pair of scissors from his coat pocket and cut the microphone cord in two. People could no longer hear the Girls' song!

The crowd looked up at Blossom, Bubbles, and Buttercup in confusion.

Then Ace plugged Fuzzy's guitar back in. "Here ya go, Fuzzy!" he called out.

So Fuzzy started to play again, but this time he had some new words.

Them Powerpuffs tried ta make
y'all stop.
Let's show 'em how ta really rock!

Git 'em! Git 'em! Git them 'puffs!
So they cain't keep botherin' us!

Suddenly, the crowd went crazy again. But this time, everyone started attacking The Powerpuff Girls!

Uh-oh, Girls! The people of Townsville are after you! What are you going to do now?

"Let's get 'em!" shouted Buttercup.

"No, Buttercup, stop!" said Blossom. "We can't beat up the innocent people of Townsville."

"They don't look so inno-cent to me," said Bubbles as an old lady hit her with an umbrella.

"It's just Fuzzy's music," said Blossom. "It makes them crazy."

"If we can't fight them, we better do something fast," said Buttercup. "Because they look pretty mad."

"Let's go back home and come up with a plan," Blossom decided. "There must be a way to make Fuzzy change his tune!"

As the Girls flew off, Fuzzy kept singing.

> *Them Powerpuffs ain't so tough!*
> *Let's just keep on smashin' stuff!*
> *Smash! Crash! Trash and bash!*

Uh-oh — it looks like Fuzzy has a smash hit on his hands!

chapter 6

Back at the Utonium household, the Professor was still smashing everything he could get his hands on. Since he had run out of things to destroy in his lab, he had moved on to the rest of the house!

Pots and pans were thrown all around the kitchen, and all of the food in the fridge had been tossed on the floor. In the den, sparks flew from the broken television, and all the stuffing had been pulled from the couch. Even the Professor's bedroom was a wreck. But where was he now?

"Our room!" shouted all three Power-puff Girls at once. And they zoomed up-stairs.

The Professor had opened the door to their room and was about to go inside!

At blinding speed, The Powerpuff Girls zipped through the open door and slammed it behind them.

"Whew!" said Buttercup. "That was a close one."

Suddenly, there was a knock on the door.

"Oh, Girls!" called the Professor. "Can I come in and smash a few things?"

"No way!" the Girls replied.

"Please?" the Professor pleaded.

"No!" they said again.

"Pretty please with sugar on top?" he asked.

"Can't you find something else to smash, Professor?" asked Buttercup.

"But there's nothing left out here except — oh, look! A nice clean bathroom!" the Professor shouted with glee. He danced down the hall to the bathroom.

"All right, Girls, let's think," said Blossom. "How can we stop Fuzzy from making everybody so crazy?"

The Powerpuff Girls sat on their bed and thought. Nobody said anything for a long time. Outside their room, the Professor's radio was blasting Smashing Lumpkins music at full volume. Blossom looked at Buttercup. Buttercup looked at Bubbles. Bubbles looked at Blossom. All three Girls scratched their heads at the same time.

Finally, Buttercup spoke. "It sure would be easier to think if the Professor's radio wasn't on so loud," she said.

"Maybe we should turn it off," said Bubbles.

"That's it!" exclaimed Blossom.

"It is?" asked Bubbles. "Wow, that was easy!"

"How is turning the Professor's radio off going to save Townsville?" asked Buttercup. "We'd have to turn off all the radios in town!"

"No, we don't," said Blossom. "We just need to turn off the radio station! Then no one can hear Fuzzy's music!"

"Sounds like a good plan to me," said Buttercup. "Now it's our turn to smash something!"

"Let's go, Girls," said Blossom. And The Powerpuff Girls took off in a streak of bright colors.

At the Townsville radio station, Blossom, Bubbles, and Buttercup each grabbed hold of the giant metal radio tower on the roof. Using their super-strength, they broke it free from the building.

Then the three Girls all grabbed the pointed top of the tower and swung it around and around and around at super-speed. The radio tower was spinning so fast that it looked like a big steel tornado in the sky.

Finally, The Powerpuff Girls let go of the tower and sent it rocketing into space.

"It looks like that takes care of Smashing Lumpkins," said Buttercup.

"Without the tower, the radio station can't broadcast his music," said Blossom. "Let's go home and see if the Professor is back to normal."

"I hope so," said Bubbles. "But do you think he'll still dance with me?"

Oh, Bubbles! You're so cute when you're worried! Well, it looks like The Powerpuff Girls will have Townsville back in tune in no time. After all, they've thought of everything — haven't they?

When The Powerpuff Girls returned home from the radio station, they were shocked to see that the Professor was still dancing to Smashing Lumpkins!

And he was in their room! Blossom's books were in tatters! Bubbles's crayons were in crumbles! Buttercup's toys were in pieces!

And the kooky Professor was dancing and singing, "Smash! Bash! Make a crash!"

"I don't understand," said Blossom. "The Professor can't be listening to the radio. We destroyed the radio tower!"

"The record store has all of Smashing Lumpkins' music on sale!" shouted the Professor. "We don't need the radio station!"

"Oh, no," said Buttercup. "What are we

going to do now? We tried everything to make Fuzzy stop! We smashed his banjo. We smashed the radio tower. There's nothing left to smash!"

"Maybe that's the problem," said Blossom. "We've been trying to solve the problem by destroying things."

"We're acting just like Smashing Lumpkins!" Bubbles realized.

"That's right, Bubbles," said Blossom. "Maybe the best way to get people to stop smashing things is to stop smashing things ourselves! Huddle up, Girls. I have an idea."

It looks like The Powerpuff Girls are going to start singing a different tune from now on! Let's hope Blossom's plan works!

chapter 7

Later that day, The Powerpuff Girls showed up at Fuzzy's cabin in the woods.

"Okay, Girls," said Blossom. "You know why we're here. Try to find all the pieces of Fuzzy's broken banjo."

"Do you really think we can fix it?" asked Bubbles.

"I hope so," said Blossom. "It might be our only hope."

"I found a banjo string," announced Buttercup.

"I think this is one of those knob thingies that goes on the end," said Bubbles.

Finally, they had collected all the pieces. Then, using glue, tape, and a little bit of superheat vision, they reconstructed Fuzzy's banjo piece by piece. When they were done, it looked as good as new!

"Good job, Girls," said Blossom. "Now let's fix the radio tower so all of Townsville can hear Fuzzy play."

Put the radio tower back! But they just threw it into space. Broadcast Fuzzy Lumpkins! But that's what was causing all the trouble in the first place! I sure hope The Powerpuff Girls know what they're doing!

Bubbles grabbed Fuzzy's banjo, and The Powerpuff Girls blasted off into space. In no time, they snatched the radio tower out of its orbit and brought it back down to Earth. They placed it right back on top of the Townsville radio station.

"Now it's time for phase three of our plan," said Blossom. "Do you still have Fuzzy's banjo, Bubbles?"

"You're darn tootin'," said Bubbles. She gave the banjo a strum.

"Then let's start the show," Buttercup shouted. And The Powerpuff Girls hurried downtown.

Fuzzy was still singing and smashing things with his electric guitar. But now the Gangreen Gang had joined Fuzzy onstage as his backup singers! They sounded worse than ever. And the crowd was acting even crazier than ever!

The Powerpuff Girls swooped down and hovered right in front of Fuzzy. He stopped singing. "The Powerpuff Girls!" he shouted. "Are y'all gonna smash ma new guitar, too? Or does y'all jus' want another whoopin' from ma fans?"

The crowd let out a cheer.

"No, Fuzzy," said Blossom. "We're not here to smash anything."

"That's right, Fuzzy," added Buttercup. "We just want to give you a present."

"A present! Fer me?" Fuzzy shouted with excitement. "Is it good fer smashin'?"

"No, silly, it's your banjo," said Bubbles and she held his banjo high in the air.

"Ma banjo! I loves ma banjo!" he ex-

claimed. Fuzzy dropped his electric guitar and grabbed the banjo from Bubbles. "Hey there, banjo, old buddy," Fuzzy said to his banjo. "I sure did miss ya."

"Now why don't you show everybody in Townsville what real Fuzzy Lumpkins music sounds like?" Blossom suggested.

"That there is a right good idear, Blossom," said Fuzzy. And he started to play his banjo and sing.

Oh, I'm as happy as a hog in sludge,
I likes ma banjo oh so much.
Them Powerpuff Girls done fixed it right,
Fer now, I guess that we won't have to fight.

Suddenly, the people in the crowd stopped smashing things. They stopped

dancing, and they started listening. And they didn't like what they heard!

"That's the worst singing I've ever heard!" shouted the Mayor. "What is he doing in front of City Hall?"

The rest of the crowd agreed with the Mayor. They thought Fuzzy's banjo music stunk. And they all walked away from City Hall holding their ears, without destroying anything.

Even the Gangreen Gang had heard enough. They turned themselves back in to the police! "Put us in a nice, quiet jail cell," Ace told the police. "We can't listen to this noise anymore."

People all over Townsville turned off their radios so they wouldn't have to listen to Fuzzy. Soon, the only noise in Townsville was Fuzzy singing his happy little song on the steps of City Hall. And his singing was worse than ever.

But The Powerpuff Girls didn't seem to mind. They were smiling! And they were dancing! To them, Fuzzy's banjo played the best music they had ever heard. Thanks to that banjo, Townsville was finally back to its normal, peaceful self.

And so, once again, the day is saved, thanks to The Powerpuff Girls!